We are beginn
tradition A.
this year &
it might be fun for
you to try it too!

Let me know who finds
the
pickle
in the
tree
&
gets
1 extra
"small" gift!

Happy "Pickle
hunting"

Love,

Aunt &
Deb &
Uncle Jim

The Legend

of the

Christmas Pickle

I would like to acknowledge Linda Fillion and Geoff Booker for all of the help and support of this book.

Preface

There have been many stories about how the Christmas pickle tradition came about. I only knew of one, my own. My name is Tony Fillion and this is the story of how the Christmas pickle tradition began in my family.

Chapter One

It was December 21, 1958, four days before Christmas. Snow was falling at night in the quiet town of Milwaukee. Some of the houses were decorated with Christmas lights. The houses had a foot of snow on the roofs. Some houses had smoke coming from the chimney from the fireplaces that kept the houses warm. The snow plow driver was busy cleaning the street of the excess snow. Christmas carolers were going door to door singing Christmas carols. Their voices were in perfect harmony and sounded like angels singing.

Among the many houses was a white house that belonged to my grandparents. The sidewalk and driveway glistened from being freshly shoveled. The house had white lights around the front windows. A large green Christmas wreath was hanging on the front door. A small snowman with a carrot nose, a black hat, and black buttons for his eyes was in the middle of the front yard made by the children that lived in the house.

My grandmother Mary Fillion, was 40 years old and a mother of three who had curly brown hair and wore glasses. She was wearing a yellow apron with pink flowers. She enjoyed cooking for her family.

Mary was in the kitchen cooking the family dinner. The kitchen was painted white with country themed decorations. There were two pots simmering on the stove. In the oven was the main dinner which filled the kitchen with its rich aroma.

Mary yelled for the children. "Kids, will you come down here?! Your cousins will be here soon!"

Sandy, a 5 year old girl, John, a 6 year old boy, and Michael, an 8 year old boy came down the wooden stairs that led into the large living room. Michael was my father.

Sandy had curly blond hair and she loved the color pink, all of her dresses were pink. She always got along with her bigger brothers.

John was the middle child. He didn't like going to school and sometimes felt left out because he didn't have many friends. He liked to play in the snow in the winter and play baseball in the summer.

Michael was protective of his younger brother and sister. He liked to help his parents around the house with the chores. He always got good grades in school and wanted to be a doctor when he got older. My dad never became a doctor. He became a general contractor instead.

The fireplace was glowing as the logs crackled. It gave the house a warm cozy feeling. There were five red stockings that represented the family members. A tan colored couch, a loveseat, and two chairs were in front of the fireplace.

The lighted Christmas tree in the corner had a lot of colorful decorations with a gold shiny star on top that made the tree complete. Underneath the tree was a red skirt with a snowflake pattern where the Christmas presents will be placed under the tree.

My grandfather Howard Fillion, was 42 years old and was in the living room reading the newspaper on the couch.

He had black short hair and only wore glasses for reading. He was slightly overweight. He was a hard worker and always provided for his family.

Mary walked into the dining room and took the fancy dinnerware out of the China cabinet that they use for special occasions.

"What were we having for dinner?" Howard asked.

"Ham with sweet potatoes and all of the fixings." Mary said.

"Mmmm, sounds delicious."

Two cars pulled up to the house. The first car parked in the street. It belonged to Edith and Richard Jones. They had three children, Jackie and Sharon, their 6 year old twins, and their older son Billy, who was 10 years old.

Edith was 35 years old and Mary's younger sister. Mary and Edith were always close growing up. They didn't have any brothers, only each other. Edith had long thin blonde hair.

Richard was 38 years old. He was a tall thin man with a thick brown mustache and straight hair. He had a tattoo on his right arm of a bald eagle.

Jackie and Sharon had blonde curly hair and wore a light blue dress with white shiny shoes.

Billy was very protective of his younger sisters. He had straight brown hair like his father.

The second car parked in the driveway. It belonged to Walter and Josephine Smith, the grandparents. They were the parents of Mary and Edith.

Walter was a thin bald short man that wore glasses. He was 65 years old. He was retired and liked to watch sports.

Josephine was a petite thin woman. She was old fashioned. She had short grey curly hair. She was wearing a light blue dress.

Mary was setting the table in the dining room. "Michael, will you help me set the table?"

"Sure Mom."

The doorbell rang.

Mary answered the door. "Hi Edith."

"Hello Mary." Edith said.

"Hi Mom. Hi Dad." Mary said.

"Hello dear." Josephine said.

"Hey Walter." Howard said

"Hello Howard." Walter said.

"Kids, now you behave yourselves." Edith said as Jackie, Sharon, and Billy ran into the house and up the stairs with Sandy, John, and Michael.

Howard said to Walter and Josephine, "Here, let me take your coats." Howard took their coats and put them in the hallway closet.

"So Mom how was the trip?" Mary asked.

"It was very exhausting dear. It was such a long ride. We need to move closer."

Josephine, Mary, and Edith went into the kitchen.

"That smells so good. You two always enjoyed cooking when you were kids." Josephine said.

"Thanks Mom." Mary said.

"What were you making?" Josephine asked.

"Ham with sweet potatoes, macaroni and cheese, green beans with bread and butter."

"Sounds delicious dear."

"Mary was always the better cook. Weren't you?" Edith asked.

"No, I think you were."

"Hey, do you remember the smell of Christmas cookies at grandma's house? Mary asked.

"Yes, the house always smelled so good." Edith said.

"Hey, we should make some cookies." Mary said.

"Sounds good." Edith said. "I'll get the ingredients out, you get the bowl."

Walter, Howard, and Richard were watching a football game on a black and white TV in the living room. The children came downstairs and ran around in the living room.

"So Howard, what's new? How's work?" Walter asked.

"They're keeping us busy. It's never ending."

Mary went into the living room with a tray of condiments which included pickles, olives, celery, onion dip, crackers and cheese, and nuts.

"Here were some snacks to munch on before dinner." Mary said to Walter, Howard, and Richard.

"Thank you dear." Howard said.

"Kids, will you stop running around before somebody got hurt." Mary said as the children continued to run around. The children ignored Mary.

"Howard, say something to them before somebody got hurt." Mary said.

"Kids, you heard her." Howard said in a firm voice.

As Mary walked past the Christmas tree, Sandy bumped into Mary and a pickle fell off the tray and landed on a branch inside the Christmas tree.

"Now look what you did!" Mary yelled.

All of the children ran into the other room.

"What happened?" Howard asked.

"One of the pickles fell off the tray and landed somewhere in the Christmas tree."

"Do you see it?" Richard asked.

Mary looked in the tree. "No, and if I don't find it, it's going to smell."

"That's okay. I'll help you look for it." Howard said.

Mary thought for a minute. "No, wait a minute, I have a better idea." Mary called the children. "Kids, will you come in here for a minute?"

The children hesitated at first but then came into the living room.

"Yes Mom?" Michael asked.

"About the pickle that fell into the tree." Mary said.

"We're sorry." Sandy said with a sad face.

"That's okay." Mary said. "I need you to look for it."

"Why do we have to look for it?" John asked. "Sandy's the one that did it."

"Well, I'll make you a deal. Whoever finds the pickle will get an extra Christmas present."

"Really? How? You don't know Santa." Sandy said.

Howard knew he had to go along with it. "Yes she does. Do you think she would lie to you about something like that?"

Sandy, John, and Michael looked at each other and started looking for the pickle. Jackie, Sharon, and Billy stood by and watched.

"Be careful and don't mess up the tree." Mary said.

After a while, Sandy found the pickle.

"I found it!! I found it!!" Sandy yelled with excitement.

John and Michael were disappointed that they didn't find the pickle but were happy for Sandy at the same time.

"Good for you!! I'm gonna go upstairs and call Santa to let him know." Mary said.

Sandy had a big grin on her face. "Thank you Mommy!"

So, the tradition of the Christmas pickle was started in my family and was passed down through the generations.

Chapter Two

It was now the present day, Friday December 23. There was a Christmas tree lot on Main Street that had many trees of different shapes and sizes. The different colored blinking lights that were hung around the lot gave it a cozy Christmas feeling.

I was driving my red Ford pickup truck with my two children, Sam and Sally. We pulled into the Christmas tree lot to pick out this year's tree.

I was 40 years old with straight brown hair that was parted in the middle. I had an athletic build. I was a general contractor and had my own business like my dad. I always looked up to my dad. He's the reason why I became a general contractor. There was a sign on my truck that advertised my business.

Sam was 10 years old and Sally was 8 years old. Sally was sitting in the middle.

Sam had straight brown hair like me. He was a thin boy. He had blue eyes and wore glasses. He always looked out for Sally.

Sally was thin like Sam. She had long blonde hair. She was always happy and enjoyed playing with Sam. She had bells on her shoelaces that jingled every time she moved her feet.

"Okay kids, were you ready to pick out this year's Christmas tree?" I asked.

"Yup. Let's get a really big tree Dad." Sam said.

Sally said, "Yeah, and we can decorate it really pretty."

"Sounds good. Let's go see what they got." I said.

We got out of the truck and walked over to the trees.

Jeff Booker, the salesman, was a large man with black hair and friendly. He was standing near a small wooden shack.

The wooden shack had Christmas lights hanging from it. There were Christmas wreaths for sale that people would hang on their front doors.

"Good afternoon folks. Can I help you?" Jeff asked.

I said, "We're looking for a Christmas tree."

"Feel free to look around and if there is something that you need, just give a holler. The name's Jeff."

"Thanks." I said.

We looked around and came up to a large light green tree. The tree looked perfect. The height was just right. All of the branches were straight where the ornaments would hang from.

"What about this one Dad?" Sally asked.

"That's a nice tree Sally. What do you think Sam?"

"It looks good to me Dad."

I walked over to Jeff. "We'll take that one." I said as I pointed to the tree.

Jeff replied, "Good choice. That will be $40."

I took out my brown wallet out of my back pocket and paid Jeff for the tree.

"Merry Christmas" Jeff said.

"Merry Christmas to you too." I said and then I turned to Sam. "Give me a hand putting it in the truck."

"Sure thing Dad."

Sam and I picked up the tree. I carried the bottom of the tree and Sam carried the top. Sam had a little trouble at first but then got the hang of it.

"Were you okay Sam?" I asked.

"Yeah, I'm okay."

Sally walked along side of the tree holding a branch pretending to help. I looked at Sally and smiled. We walked up to the truck. I pulled the tailgate down and we put the tree in the back of the truck and drove home.

Chapter Three

I pulled up to my white cottage house that had black shutters and a one car garage. There was a blue minivan parked in front of the house that belonged to my wife Beverly. There were small bushes in front of the house. There were toys scattered in the front yard. There were candy cane pinwheels in the front yard. The kids always enjoyed them. They liked how colorful the pinwheels were when they spun. There was a snow gauge near the house to measure the snow that was shaped like a snowman with a ruler alongside of it. There was also a reindeer crossing sign and a street sign that said Candy Cane Lane. In the windows were lights that were shaped like angels, bells, and candy canes.

I backed the truck up in the driveway and stopped a few feet away from the garage door. Sam and I took the tree out of the back of the truck and placed it on the ground. I opened the garage door.

"Sally, can you get the inside door?" I asked.

Sally smiled. "Sure Daddy."

Sally walked over to the door that led from the garage into the house and held the door open as Sam and I brought the Christmas tree into the house to the living room.

The living room had brown shag carpet with light brown furniture. There was an empty space in one of the corners for the Christmas tree. There was a Snowman Door Drafter at the front door to prevent drafts that came under the door. There were Christmas cards hanging on the wall from friends and family. On the main wall of the living room was the fireplace. Candy cane stocking holders held the stockings in place. On the mantle was a clock. A couple of years ago I bought a Dancing snowman for Sally. When you pushed the button, a song played and the snowman danced and sung. She always smiled every time the snowman danced. I kept it on the coffee table for all to see.

My wife Beverly was in the living room. She was 38 years old and had long blonde hair with a thin figure. She was wearing blue jeans and a light blue T-shirt that she always wore when she worked or cleaned around the house.

Coco, out brown terrier dog, was lying next to her. Sam and I walked into the living room with the Christmas tree. Sally was walking behind us.

"Sally, Coco missed you today." Beverly said.

Coco wagged his tail as Sally came over and sat next to him. "Hi Coco."

"So, what do you think Beverly?" I asked.

"I picked it out." Sally said as she petted Coco.

"Wow Sally, that's a beautiful tree." Beverly said.

"Sam, can you help me bring down the decorations from the attic?" I asked.

"Sure Dad." Sam said.

Sam and I walked over to a rectangle opening in the ceiling in the main hallway that had collapsible stairs. I pulled on the string that was hanging down and pulled down the collapsible stairs. Sam and I climbed the stairs up to the attic. In the attic were many boxes.

"It sure is dirty up here. It's hard to find anything." Sam said.

"A lot of this stuff was collected over the years. There were a lot of memories in these boxes." I said.

I looked around for the boxes of decorations. They were in the back corner labeled in black magic marker, "Christmas Decorations".

"Ah, here they were." I said.

Sam and I grabbed the boxes and brought them down to the living room. The boxes contained elves, snowmen, and sled ornaments.

The male elves had red suits and the female elves had green suits. There was another box that had strands of multi-colored lights that were rolled up. There were also two boxes of silver garland.

Sam and I placed the boxes in front of the Christmas tree.

"Dad, where do you want these?" Sam asked.

"Put them over by the tree." I said.

"Okay Dad." Sam said.

"Sam, give me a hand with these lights. They have to go on first." I said.

"Okay." Sam said.

Sam and I took the lights out of the boxes and began putting the lights on the tree. When we were done, I plugged the lights in and the lights blinked and lit up the living room.

"Wow that looks really good." Beverly said.

Sam and I looked at each other and smiled knowing that we did a good job.

"Okay, time for the garland. Sally, do you want to help me put the garland on the tree?" Beverly asked.

"Yes Mommy." Sally said.

Beverly put the silver garland on the tree and Sally held the slack. When they were finished, the silver garland sparkled as the Christmas lights shined upon it.

"Wow that looks really good. The only thing left were the ornaments." Beverly said.

Beverly, Sam, Sally, and I started putting the ornaments on the tree. When Sam reached into one of the boxes, he found a Christmas pickle ornament.

"Dad, there's a pickle ornament in here." Sam said.

"Here, give me that. I'll take care of it." I said.

Sam handed me the Christmas pickle ornament.

"For a minute there, I thought it was gonna go on the tree." Sam said.

"It is." I said.

"What do you mean? Pickles don't have anything to do with Christmas." Sam said.

"Sure they do. The pickle is the last ornament that's hidden inside the tree." I said.

"Dad, why would you hide a pickle in the tree?" Sam asked.

"On Christmas morning, whoever finds it got an extra present." I said.

"Really?" Sally asked.

I waved Sam and Sally to sit by the fire. I held the pickle out and spun it in my hand as I talked.

"Yeah, the legend of the pickle went like this. To start a tradition that will surely last, here's the story about the pickle of glass. The night before Christmas it's hung on the tree. While everyone's sleeping, it's done secretly. On Christmas morning when you arise, the first one to find it will get a surprise. A family tradition for all to share, you'll look for the pickle year after year." I said.

"Daddy, did you look for the Christmas pickle when you were a kid?" Sally asked.

"Yes, it's been in my family for years." I said.

"What about you Mommy?" Sally asked.

"No, just your father." Beverly said.

"Well, I think you kids were old enough now to start doing it this year." I said.

"Cool, I'm gonna find it first." Sam said.

"No you're not, I am." Sally said.

"Okay kids, stop fighting. It's supposed to be a fun thing. C'mon, let's finish putting on the rest of the ornaments." I said.

I put the Christmas pickle ornament off to the side. Beverly, Sam, Sally, and I finished decorating the tree. I put the white star on the top of the tree and plugged it into the Christmas tree lights. The white star lit up and made the Christmas tree complete.

"Wow what a beautiful tree. You picked out a really nice one." Beverly said.

"Something's missing." I said.

"What?" Beverly asked.

"Oh I know! The train set!" Sam said.

"Yup." I said.

I looked through the boxes and found the train set. "Sam, help me set it up."

"Okay Dad." Sam said.

"Sally, do you want to help?" I asked.

"Sure."

Sam, Sally, and I put the train set together and placed it under the tree. It had a black engine and four cars with a caboose.

"Okay Sam, turn it on." I said.

Sam turned the switch on the black engine and the train began to go around the tree. Smoke came out of the top of the engine. There was a stone colored tunnel for the train to go through. The controls for the train had a button for the whistle to blow.

"Now the tree is complete. Hey, I got an idea. What do you say we go to the mall?" I asked.

"Cool. Can I play at the arcade?" Sam asked.

"We'll see." Beverly said.

"I want to see Santa Claus!" Sally said.

"Sally, did you write your letter to Santa?" Beverly asked.

"Yes, we did it in school." Sally said.

"Why don't you go to your room and get it so you can give it to Santa Claus?" Beverly asked.

"Okay." Sally said. Sally went up to her room and got the letter that she wrote for Santa and came back down the stairs in a hurry.

"Okay, let's go." I said.

As I walked toward the front door, Beverly stopped him as she stood in front of me.

"What's the matter?" I asked.

"Look." Beverly pointed to the mistletoe above my head.

"In that case." I grabbed Beverly and gave her a kiss. "Okay, let's go."

Beverly, Sam, Sally, and I got in Beverly's blue minivan and drove to the Middletown Mall.

Chapter Four

On the way to the mall, we drove by a large Christmas tree that stood in the center of town. The tree had thousands of colorful lights that blinked. There were silver and gold ball ornaments that shined from the Christmas lights. A shiny gold star was on top of the tree that made it complete.

"Dad, can we stop and take a picture of the tree?" Sam asked.

"Yeah, can we Dad?" Sally asked.

"Sure, why not." I pulled over and we got out of the minivan. "Okay, you guys stand in front of the tree." I said.

"What about you Daddy?" Sally asked.

I saw Robert Jackson, a retired store owner walking towards me.

"Excuse me sir but could you be so kind and take a picture of me and my family?" I asked.

"Sure, I'd be happy to." Robert said.

I handed Robert my camera and walked over to the tree where Beverly, Sam, and Sally were standing. Beverly and I stood behind Sam and Sally.

"Ready?" Robert asked.

"Ready." I said.

Robert made sure that all of us were in the picture and then took our picture.

"Thank you." I said.

"You're welcome." Robert handed me the camera back and left.

"Merry Christmas." I said.

"Merry Christmas to you too." Robert said.

Robert walked away. Beverly, Sam, Sally, and I got back into the minivan and headed for the mall.

As we drove down Washington Avenue, we came across Midtown Park. There were hills and mounds of snow. There were children on sleds going down a hill. A group of parents by the lake were watching the children ice skate on the small pond.

In the middle of the park was a gazebo. A loud speaker was playing Christmas music. The roof and railing of the gazebo was covered with snow. There was a newlywed couple, Tom and Apryl Dunnley inside the gazebo.

Apryl was 30 years old with short brown hair. She was wearing a white fur coat with a matching fur muff and hat.

Tom was 31 years old with short black hair. He was a tall handsome thin man.

"Isn't this romantic?" Tom asked as he looked into Apryl's eyes.

"Yes it is. It reminds me of our first date when we went skiing." Apryl said.

Apryl moved towards Tom and gave him a kiss. They held hands and watched the snow fall. After a while they left the gazebo.

As they walked along the snow covered walkway, Tom picked up some snow and threw it at Apryl. As Tom ran up to Apryl, she picked up some snow and threw it at Tom. They laughed and enjoyed their time playing in the snow.

At the entrance of the park, were signs for sleigh rides. There were three horses with sleighs waiting for people to ride on.

Kenny and Stephanie Lamont walked up to the sleigh rides with their son, Joey. They were residents of Milwaukee.

Kenny was 35 years old. He had short hair and thin. He enjoyed playing golf.

Stephanie was 34 years old. She was shorter than Kenny and had long brown hair. She enjoyed exercising and staying fit.

Joey was 12 years old. He had short hair and tall like his father. He was very energetic and loved playing outside.

Peter Daine, a 45 year old salesman, was dressed in a top hat and a fine gray long coat with black strap boots. His smile was full of genuine holiday spirit as he shook a leather strap with golden jingle bells on it.

"How much for the sleigh ride?" Kenny asked.

"$20 for a half hour ride." Peter said.

Kenny turned to Stephanie. "Do you want to go for a ride?"

"Sure. Joey, do you want to go on a sleigh ride with me and your father?" Stephanie asked.

"I would rather go sledding." Joey said.

"I don't know. That looks steep." Kenny said.

Joey whined. "Mom, please?"

"I don't know." Stephanie said.

"Well, the right side of the hill is a nice ride for kids. It's not too steep. I can loan him my sled while you folks go on a sleigh ride." Peter said.

"Is it safe to leave them by themselves?" Kenny asked.

"Yes. I have people that work for me that will watch them." Peter said.

"Okay, that sounds good. Joey, make sure that you stay on the right side of the hill away from the big kids." Kenny said.

"Okay Dad." Joey said.

Kenny and Stephanie got into the sleigh and went for a ride and Joey got the sled and went sledding.

Sam pressed his face up against the window. "Wow that looks fun!"

"Maybe we'll stop on the way back." I said as I thought it would be fun as well. I remembered when I was young when I used to go sledding.

"Yeah, you kids can go sledding while your father and I go on a sleigh ride." Beverly said.

"That sounds really nice." I said even though I would rather go sledding with Sam.

Chapter Five

Beverly, Sam, and Sally, and I pulled up to the Middletown Mall. It was a large two story light brown brick building. The parking lot was mostly full. We drove around for a while and finally found a parking spot.

As we walked towards the main entrance, Mike Rivers was standing outside ringing a gold bell with a black handle. He was 50 years old. He was thin with brown hair and had a mustache and beard. He was wearing a black coat and hat. He was collecting money for charity. I put a five dollar bill in the basket.

"Thank you. Merry Christmas." Mike said.

"Merry Christmas." I said.

Beverly, Sam, Sally, and I went inside the mall. Christmas music was playing throughout the mall. The stores were decorated with green and red Christmas lights and decorations.

"Daddy, why did you give that man outside money?" Sally asked.

"Because it's better to give then receive." I said.

"I don't understand." Sally said.

"You will someday." I grabbed and held Sally's hand. We walked past several different stores. Every store was busy with people doing their last minute shopping. There were signs in the windows advertising Christmas sales.

In the middle of the mall was an area called the North Pole. Children could get their picture taken with Santa Claus. There was artificial snow on the ground with artificial trees and bushes. There were two fake reindeers standing in the artificial snow.

Jim Frederick played Santa Claus every year at the mall. He was a local resident and lived down the street from us. He was an Army Sergeant and got a purple heart a few years ago. He loved to help people and volunteer for good causes, especially at Christmas. He was a heavy set man with the perfect body to play Santa Claus. He dyed his hair white for Christmas and wore a red Santa Claus suit with a white trim, a fake long white beard and a thick shiny black belt. He sat in a chair large enough for him and a child that would sit on his lap telling him what they wanted for Christmas.

The elves that helped Santa with the children were short and had pointed ears. They wore green costumes with green hats and red curly shoes. Sally and I walked up to the entrance to the North Pole.

"Daddy, those elves look like the ones we have on our tree." Sally said.

"Yes they do. C'mon, let's get in line." I said.

"Okay." Sally said.

"Sam, did you want to see Santa Claus too?" I asked.

"No, that's okay. Can I go to the arcade?" Sam asked.

"Only if your mother went with you." I said.

"Sure, why not." Beverly said.

"Thanks Mom." Sam said.

Beverly and Sam went to the arcade nearby. Sally and I got in line to see Santa Claus.

Flake the elf camera man was getting ready to take a picture when all of a sudden the camera broke.

Zippy, one of the elves that helped with the children was standing next to him.

"You know, if Santa's elves would have built this camera, it wouldn't have broken so easily." Flake said.

"You got that right." Zippy said.

After a while Flake fixed the camera. "Okay, I got it."

There were five children in front of Sally.

Lisa, a small girl is sitting on Santa's lap.

"And what would you like for Christmas?" Santa asked.

"I would like a new doll house Santa." Lisa said.

"Okay. I'll see what I can do. Have you been a good girl?" Santa asked.

"Yes Santa." Lisa said.

"Okay. Smile for the camera." Santa said.

Flake took their picture. Lisa got down from Santa's lap.

Frank, a small boy got on Santa's lap with the help of one of the elves.

"Well hello there young man. What's your name?" Santa asked.

"Frank."

"Have you been a good boy Frank?"

"Yes Santa."

"Let me check my naughty list." Santa looked at the naughty list. "Okay, I don't see your name. What would you like for Christmas?" Santa asked.

"I like to play football. Can I get a football?" Frank asked.

"You're a little small to handle a real football. How about a foam one?" Santa asked.

"I don't know." Frank said.

"Do you want something you can enjoy now or something you'll have to wait a few years to grow into it?" Santa asked.

"You mean like auntie's sweater?" Frank asked.

"Yup." Santa said.

"Okay, the foam is good then." Frank said.

"Smart man. Sometimes getting what you want isn't as good as getting what you need." Santa said.

"Thanks Santa." Frank said.

"Now let's take our picture together." Santa said.

"Okay, smile for the camera." Flake took their picture.

Frank got down from Santa's lap.

Charlie, a small boy got on Santa's lap.

"Hello there. What's your name?"

"Charlie."

"And what would you like for Christmas?" Santa asked.

"A telescope."

"Can I ask why do you want a telescope?" Santa asked.

"I want to be an astronaut someday." Charlie said.

"Okay Charlie, I'll do what I can." Santa said.

"Thanks Santa." Charlie said.

"You're welcome. Were you ready to get your picture taken with Santa?" Santa asked.

"Can my mom be in the picture?" Charlie asked.

"Sure." Santa said.

"Mom, Santa said you get can get your picture taken with us." Charlie said.

Charlie's mother walked over to Santa and Charlie and stood on the side of the chair next to Charlie.

"Okay, ready?" Flake asked. Flake saw that they were ready and snapped a photo.

"Thanks Santa." Charlie said.

"You're welcome. Merry Christmas." Santa said.

The elves helped Charlie get down from Santa's lap. Linda, a small girl got up on Santa's lap.

"Hello young lady and what's your name?" Santa asked.

"Linda."

"That's a lovely name. Have you been good this year?" Santa asked.

"Mama says I have."

"And what would you like for Christmas?"

"An easy light oven." Linda said.

"I think I can do that." Santa said.

"Do you think Mrs. Claus can put a recipe with it for cookies?" Linda asked.

"What type of cookie?" Santa asked.

"The chocolate ones with the cream in the center. You know, the ones you dunk in milk." Linda said.

"Nope, can't do that." Santa said.

"Really? I thought you can do anything." Linda said.

"I can do a lot but I wouldn't take a recipe that's not hers. She makes really good chocolate chip cookies though." Santa said.

"My mom makes really good chocolate chip cookies too." Linda said.

"Yes, I remember. You left them out for me last year." Santa said.

"You're right, we did." Linda said.

"I think you should stick to the chocolate chip cookies." Santa said.

"Okay. Thanks Santa. Merry Christmas." Linda said.

"You're welcome. Merry Christmas to you too. Before you go, let's take your picture, okay?" Santa asked.

"Okay." Linda said.

Santa gave Flake a signal to take their picture.

"Smile!" Flake took their picture.

The elves helped Linda get down from Santa's lap. Dave was next in line. The elves helped Dave get up on Santa's lap.

"Hello. What's your name?" Santa asked.

"Dave."

"Were you a good boy this year?" Santa asked.

"Yes."

"Let me check my naughty list." Santa checked the naughty list. "I don't see your name. What would you like for Christmas?

"A new toy truck." Dave said.

"A new toy truck it is." Dave said.

"Thanks Santa." Dave said.

"Do you want your picture taken with Santa?" Santa asked.

"Yes Santa." Dave said.

"Smile for the camera." Santa said.

Flake took their picture. The elves helped Dave get down from Santa's lap. It was now Sally's turn. She walked up to Santa and one of the elves helped Sally onto Santa's lap.

"And what's your name little girl?" Santa asked.

"Sally. I wrote you a letter in school." Sally handed Santa the letter.

"Thank you. Have you been a good girl?" Santa asked.

"Yes I have." Sally said.

"That's good because I'd know if you've been naughty or nice." Santa said.

"I know. I've been extra good this year." Sally said.

Santa pulled out a list with names on it. "Let me check the naughty list." Santa looked it over. Santa then looked at it a second time.

The flash on the camera went off.

"Flake, we weren't ready. Do you want me to put you on the naughty list?" Santa asked.

"Sorry Santa, it slipped." Flake said.

Santa looked at Sally. "Sorry about that. Well, I don't see your name on the list anywhere so that means that you were good this year. So, tell Santa what you would like for Christmas." Santa said.

"I would like a new bicycle for me and my brother. I wrote it in my letter." Sally said.

Santa looked over at me and I nodded my head at Santa.

"Okay. I'll do my best." Santa said.

"Were you ready Santa?" Flake asked.

"Yes Flake, you can take the picture." Santa said.

"Okay, smile for the picture!" Flake said.

Santa and Sally looked at the camera. Flake took their picture.

"He's pretty weird." Sally whispered to Santa.

"Thanks Sally. I was thinking the same thing all afternoon." Santa whispered back to Sally.

Santa smiled as he picked up Sally from his lap and put her on the floor. Sally smiled back at Santa.

"Thank you Santa." Sally said.

"You're welcome. Don't forget your picture." Santa said.

Sally walked over to me.

"Did you have fun with Santa?" I asked,

"Yes I did. I asked him for new bikes for Sam and me." Sally said.

"Maybe Santa will get it for you." I said.

Sally looked up at me and smiled. We walked over to the register and I paid for the picture. Beverly and Sam exited the arcade and walked over to Sally and me.

"Hey Sam, I asked Santa for new bicycles for both of us!" Sally said.

"I hope we get them. Ours were old." Sam said.

"Me too! Look, I also got my picture taken with Santa." Sally showed Beverly and Sam.

"That's very nice dear. We'll hang it on the refrigerator when we get home." Beverly said.

Beverly, Sam, Sally, and I left the North Pole and began to walk through the mall.

"I hope Santa will keep his promise." Sally said.

"I'm sure he will." I said as I smirked at Beverly.

We continued to walk through the mall and walked up to a Christmas store.

The Christmas store had a village displayed in the front window. There was a Christmas Clock Tower, a Gingerbread House, a Bakery, a Pancake House, a Christmas Shop, Santa's Workshop, a toy store, people ice skating in the park, a church, a Candy and Gift Shop, a Coffee and Cocoa Shop, different houses, a Ski and Skate Shop, and a Bed and Breakfast. Christmas Carolers were singing in the street next to the black lamp posts that line the street. Some of the buildings were animated. There was a train track that circled the village.

"Look at all the cool stuff." Sam said.

"Let's go check it out." I said.

We went inside the Christmas store and walked around.

The store had Christmas ornaments and lights for sale. There were artificial Christmas trees with different ornaments on display which were set up with different themes. There were display cases with different snow globes all over the store.

There were stuffed animals and toys for all ages. They had coffee mugs, jingle bells, candy cane pens and pencils, peppermint candy shaped clocks, gingerbread house kits, candy, lollipops, costumes, wrapping paper and boxes, and Christmas cards. They had elf and Santa costumes and wreaths. They had Peppermint candy yo-yo's, pin the nose on the snowman game, peg games, kazoos, and bendable characters of snowmen, elves, Santa, and even a gingerbread man. They even had a Reindeer back scratcher. As we walked through the store, Beverly saw some Christmas jewelry.

"Wow, this is pretty. This would be nice to wear for Christmas." Beverly said.

"Maybe Santa will get it for you. Mommy, you should ask him." Sally said.

Beverly smiled at me. "I'm sure he already knows sweetie."

"I'm sure he does." I made a mental note in my head what to get Beverly. The children were always easy but not Beverly. She's always picky about things.

As I walked through the store, I saw the Christmas pickle ornaments for sale. "Hey Sam, look, they have Christmas pickle ornaments for sale."

"Are we gonna get another one?" Sam asked.

"No, you only need one. Why would you want another one? Did you think that you would get an extra present?" I asked.

"Sure, why not?" Sam asked.

I shook my head and smiled. Sam saw a display of mistletoe for sale.

"Hey Dad, what's a mistletoe?" Sam asked.

"It's another legend about Christmas like the Christmas pickle." I said.

"What do you mean?" Sam asked.

"Mistletoe is one of the most famous symbols of Christmas. It's used for Christmas decorations and it is also believed that the plant can protect the house from lightening and fire. There is also a traditional belief that if someone is standing under the Mistletoe, they would get a kiss. It's a sign of love and friendship." I explained.

"Ewww. So if I'm standing under it, a girl would kiss me." Sam said.

"Yes. That's why I kissed your mom by the front door before we left. It was hanging near the hallway." I said.

"No thank you." Sam said.

"You'll understand someday." I said.

Beverly, Sam, Sally, and I left the Christmas store and continued to walk through the mall.

As we walked by the food court, we see John and Linda Smith. Beverly and I went to school with them. John and Linda were high school sweethearts.

John was 40 years old with short brown hair. He was a stocky muscular man. He played football in high school. John and I graduated high school together.

Linda was 38 years old with short curly brown hair and wore glasses. She was a cheerleader in high school.

"What's going on Fillion?!" John asked.

"Nuffin!" Linda said.

"Yo, what's up John? You could never resist the, what's going on Fillion thing, could you?" I asked.

"Nope. Hey Bev, were these your kids?" John asked.

"Yeah, this is Sam and this is Sally. Kids, this is John and Linda." Beverly said.

"Hi." Sam said.

"Hi." Sally said.

"They're so adorable." Linda said.

"So, you guys out shopping?" I asked.

"Yeah, just picking up some last minute stuff." John said.

"Cool. Good seeing you guys. Give me a call sometime." I said.

"Will do Fillion." John said.

John and Linda left. Beverly, Sam, Sally, and I continued walking through the mall. After a while, we arrived at a toy store.

We went into the toy store and looked around. I found a truck for a boy and a doll for a girl. We walked up to the register. I placed the toys on the counter.

"Will that be all, sir?" the cashier asked.

"Yes." I said.

The cashier rang up the two toys. "That will be $22."

I handed the cashier a credit card. The cashier swiped the credit card and printed out the receipt. I signed the slip.

"Thank you." I said.

We left the cashier and as we got to the door, I put the toys in a bin labeled "Toy Drive". We left the toy store and walked through the mall.

"Daddy, why did you buy toys and then give them away?" Sally asked.

"They're for children that don't have any toys." I said.

"Were they bad? Is that why Santa won't bring them presents?" Sally asked.

"No, they're good kids. It's just that Santa is so busy this year that he can't bring presents to everyone so we help Santa out." I explained.

"Does everyone help out Santa?" Sally asked.

"Not as many as there should be." I grabbed Sally's hand and held it tight because I knew where her heart was.

"Were you guys ready to go home?" Beverly asked.

"Yeah, I think we're ready." I said.

As we walked out to the parking lot, it began to snow. We enjoyed the beautiful night as we drove home.

Chapter Six

The blue minivan pulled into the driveway. Beverly, Sam, Sally, and I exited the minivan and went inside. Sam and I went into the living room. Beverly and Sally went into the kitchen.

Sam and I were sitting on the couch watching a football game together.

"I hope the game is a good one." I said.

"Me too." Sam said.

"Hey, why don't you go in the kitchen and get the bag of chips?" I asked.

"Okay." Sam went to the kitchen.

Beverly and Sally were in the kitchen. Sam went into the kitchen.

"Hey Sam, how's the game?" Beverly asked.

"Good. Dad wants the bag of chips." Sam said.

"Okay, hold on." Beverly went into the kitchen cabinets and took out a bag of chips. "Here."

"Thanks Mom." Sam said.

"Hey Sam, while you're in there, can you get me a beer?" I asked.

"Sure Dad." Sam said.

"Thanks." I said.

Sam went into the refrigerator and got a beer then went back into the living room.

"Here you go Dad." Sam said as he gave me the beer and bag of chips then sat down on the couch next to me.

"Thanks." I said.

Beverly and Sally were sitting at the kitchen table.

"Mommy, do you know how to make snowflakes?" Sally asked,

"Sure, why?" Beverly asked.

"We need some to decorate the house with." Sally said.

"Okay, go get the white paper in your room and I'll show you." Beverly said.

"Okay." Sally went up to her room and got the white paper that was on her wooden desk and went back downstairs. Sally gave Beverly the paper. "Here you go Mommy."

"Okay, let me show you. You fold the paper a couple of times like this." Beverly folded the paper a few times. "And then cut the corners with scissors like this." Beverly cut the corners. "And when it unfolds, it looks like a snowflake." Beverly unfolded the paper to reveal a snowflake. "See."

"Can I try?" Sally asked.

"Sure." Beverly gave Sally a piece of paper and children's scissors.

Sally folded the paper five times. "How's this Mommy?"

"That's good now cut the corners but not too much." Beverly said.

Sally cut three of the corners and then unfolded the paper. "My snowflake came out pretty good Mommy."

"Yes it did. Why don't you hang it up on the refrigerator?" Beverly asked.

Sally walked over to the refrigerator and put the snowflake on the refrigerator next to her picture with Santa with a magnet. Sally was proud of her snowflake. Beverly cleaned the kitchen table off of the scrap papers leftover from the snowflakes.

"Mommy, can we make the gingerbread house and some cookies?" Sally asked.

"Sure, we'll make the gingerbread house first and then we'll make the cookies." Beverly said.

"Okay." Sally said.

Beverly opened up a cabinet in the kitchen and took down the gingerbread house kit. Beverly put the house together and Sally put the candy decorations on the house.

Sally brought the gingerbread house into the living room and put it on an end table.

"How does it look Daddy?" Sally asked.

"It looks so good that I want to eat it." I said jokingly.

"You can't eat it Daddy, it's for decoration." Sally said.

"Yeah but it looks so yummy." I said.

"Promise me you won't eat it." Sally said.

"Okay I promise." I said as he smiled.

"Thanks Daddy." Sally went back into the kitchen.

Beverly went into a drawer and took out the elf shaped cookie cutters. The cookie dough was already on the table.

"Were you ready to make the cookies?" Beverly asked.

"Yes Mommy." Sally said.

Beverly flattened out the dough and cut out the elf shaped cookies. She put them on a cookie tray and put them in the oven. When they were done, Sally decorated them.

Chapter Seven

George Klinger, his wife Margaret, and their daughter Amy lived next door to us. They had a large three bedroom white house with a chain linked fence around the property. There was a two car garage attached to the house. A white Mercedes Benz and a blue BMW were in the driveway. There was a Nativity scene in the front yard.

George and Margaret were in the living room.

George was a 45 year old tall thin man with black hair. He only wore glasses for reading. He was a successful clean cut lawyer who always dressed nice.

Margaret was 40 years old. She had short curly brown hair. She was a little overweight. She was always involved with Amy's school activities.

The large living room had a fireplace with stockings that hung from the fireplace mantle. On top of the fireplace mantle were nutcracker statues that stood about a foot high. Off to the side was an Advent calendar on a wooden table. There was a tan sectional couch with a large television in front of it. There were Poinsettia plants on the end tables. A large area rug is in the middle of the floor. A square wooden coffee table was in the middle of the sectional couch with decorative scented pine cones in a bowl.

"I'm gonna go out to the garage and get the Christmas tree and decorations." George said.

"Okay George." Margaret said.

George went into his garage to get their artificial white Christmas tree and decorations that were in boxes. He made several trips back and forth to his living room.

Amy was outside making a snowman. She was wearing a pink hat and scarf that matched her gloves with a white winter coat. Her black boots made small imprints in the snow. Amy was 10 years old and went to the same school as Sam. She was the cute little girl next door. She had long brown hair that was parted in the middle and always wore a dress. She always got good grades in school.

Margaret was in the living room looking out the window watching the snow fall as Amy built her snowman.

"That's the last box of Christmas decorations." George said.

George placed the last box on the floor. Margaret walked to the front door and opened the door.

"Amy, it's time to decorate the Christmas tree!" Margaret yelled.

"Okay Mommy, I'm coming!"

Amy ran into the house. George put the artificial white Christmas tree up in the living room. It already had blue lights on the tree.

"How does it look Margaret?" George asked.

"It looks very nice George." Margaret said.

"Can we decorate the tree now?" Amy asked.

"Sure. George, would you like some eggnog before we start?" Margaret asked.

"No that's okay." George said.

Margaret and Amy started to decorate the tree with nutcracker ornaments and silver tinsel. The nutcracker ornaments had red uniforms and their skin was tan colored.

"Daddy, where do nutcrackers come from?" Amy asked.

"Well, the story went like this. A long time ago, there was a farmer who offered a reward to anyone who could help him crack the walnuts that grew on his tree. One day a puppet maker came along with a beautiful puppet, made of wood and painted in bright colors, which had strong jaws that could be used to crack the walnuts. The farmer rewarded him by giving him his own workshop. It is also said that nutcrackers bring good luck and protect the house. They come in different colors and sizes. People use them mostly for pecans and hazelnuts." George said.

"Wow, can I get a big one for my room?" Amy asked.

"We'll see." Margaret said.

"Mommy, why don't we have a real tree for Christmas?" Amy asked.

"They're too messy Amy, and the one we have is much nicer." Margaret said.

"I think that the real trees look nice and the nutcrackers would look better on a real tree." Amy said.

"I'm sure they would dear. Oh, by the way George, we got a Christmas card from your brother today. I hung it up next to the other ones." Margaret said.

"Okay. Did you send him one as well?" George asked.

"Yes, I sent it out the other day." Margaret said.

"Good." George said.

"He also invited us to his New Year's Eve party." Margaret said.

"That's fine. We'll go." George said.

"What about Amy? Can your mother watch her?" Margaret asked.

"I'm sure she can but I'll call her to make sure." George said.

Margaret and Amy finished putting the decorations on the tree.

"That's all of the decorations. George, all that's left is the angel." Margaret said.

George put the angel on top of the tree. "Now that's a beautiful tree."

"Yes it is." Margaret said.

Whiskers, their black and silver tabby cat started playing with the Christmas lights by pulling on them.

"Whiskers! Leave that alone!! Shoo!" Margaret yelled.

Whiskers ran into the other room.

"Mommy, why does Whiskers keep trying to take things?" Amy asked.

"I don't know dear. I guess it's a cat thing." Margaret said.

Whiskers stood by the front door and meowed.

"I'm going to go out and shovel the driveway." George said.

"Okay. Can you let Whiskers out?" Margaret asked.

"Sure." George said.

George opened the door and let Whiskers outside and walked outside behind him. Whiskers walked through his yard over to ours.

Whiskers walked up to our house. There was snow on the ground with frozen puddles in the back yard. Some of Sam's toys were in the backyard. There were monster trucks, Tonka trucks, and fire trucks scattered around the yard. There were two rusty bikes lying on the ground next to the house.

Whiskers entered our house through the doggy door into the kitchen. The doggy door had jingle bells attached to it. When Whiskers entered the house, the jingle bells made noise. There was a blue dog bowl on the floor with the name "Coco" written on it. Whiskers walked up to the dog bowl and began to eat the dry dog food that was in the bowl. Coco, a black mutt, went into the kitchen and saw Whiskers eating his food and started chasing him.

Whiskers ran into the living room and went up the Christmas tree and knocked off a glass ornament. The ornament fell to the ground and broke into pieces. Coco was standing in front of the tree barking at Whiskers. Sam ran into the living room and saw Whiskers in the Christmas tree.

"Dad, the cat's in the house again!" Sam yelled as he grabbed Coco.

I went into the living room and helped chase Whiskers outside. "C'mon, get!"

Whiskers ran out through the doggy door. As he ran through our backyard, he jumped over Sam's toys like it was an obstacle course.

I went outside and saw George in the front of his house shoveling his driveway.

"Hey Tony." George said.

"Hey George. Listen, your cat was just inside my house again." I said.

"I'm sorry. Sometimes he's hard to control." George said.

"He broke one of my ornaments." I said.

"I'll pay for it. I'm really sorry." George said and pulled out his wallet and gave me money for the ornament.

"Thanks. I understand how animals can be. They have a mind of their own." I said.

"Yes they do." George said.

"Hey, do you need help shoveling the driveway?" I asked.

"No thank you. I got it." George said.

"Okay." I went back inside my house.

Chapter Eight

It was Saturday December 24, Christmas Eve. George was in the living room watching television. Margaret walked into the living room.

"Would you like something to snack on dear?" Margaret asked.

"Actually I would. Do we have any nuts?" George asked.

"Yes we do. I'll go get them." Margaret went into the kitchen and got a bag of almonds and a bowl out of a cabinet. She opened one of the drawers and got a metal nutcracker. Margaret brought the almonds and bowl out to George. "Here you go."

"Thank you. Are you gonna have some too?" George asked.

"Sure." Margaret sat down next to George and started to eat the almonds. "What were you watching?"

"It's an old western movie." George said.

"I like western movies." Margaret said.

George and Margaret watched the movie and ate the almonds. After a while, the movie was over.

"So what do you think? Good movie?" George asked.

"Yes, that was a good movie." Margaret said.

"Yup. There's nothing like a good old western to relax you." George said. "Are you ready to go to bed?"

"Yes but I want to put some cookies out for Santa. You know that Amy would get upset if I didn't put them out for Santa." Margaret said.

"Okay." George said.

Margaret went into the kitchen and opened one of the cabinets and got a box of chocolate chip cookies. She poured some cookies on a plate and brought them out in the living room. Margaret put the plate of cookies on the coffee table next to the almonds. "Were you ready to go to bed now?"

George saw the almonds still on the table. "What about the almonds?"

"I'll put them away tomorrow. It's not like they're going anywhere." Margaret said.

"True. I'm gonna check to make sure that the doors were locked." George said.

"Okay. Can you let Whiskers in while you're at it?" Margaret asked.

"Sure." George went to the front door and yelled for Whiskers. "Here Whiskers!" George waited for a while and called him again. "Here Whiskers!" George waited for a while but Whiskers still didn't come to the door.

"If he's not coming then just leave him out there. He'll be fine." Margaret said.

"Okay." George closed the front door and locked it. George and Margaret went up the stairs to their bedroom.

Chapter Nine

Beverly, Sam, Sally, and I were in the living room. There was a fire in the fireplace. Sam and Sally were under blankets snuggled up on the couch in between Beverly and me. Coco was lying on a pillow in front of the fireplace.

"Are you guys ready for T'was the night before Christmas?" I asked.

"Yeah!" Sam and Sally yelled.

"I guess that answers your question." Beverly said.

I got up from the couch and walked over to the bookshelf and got the book and then sat back down on the couch. I opened the book and began to read the book out loud.

"Twas the night before Christmas, when all through the house. Not a creature was stirring, not even a mouse. The stockings were hung by the chimney with care, in hopes that Saint Nicholas soon would be there. The children were nestled all snug in their beds. While visions of sugar-plums danced in their heads. And mama in her kerchief, and I in my cap, had just settled our brains for a long winter's nap. When out on the lawn there arose such a clatter, I sprang from the bed to see what was the matter.

Away to the window I flew like a flash, tore open the shutters and threw up the sash. The moon on the breast of the new fallen snow, gave the lustre of mid-day to objects below. When, what to my wondering eyes should appear, but a miniature sleigh, and eight tiny reindeer." I said.

Beverly looked over at Sam and Sally and noticed that they fell asleep. "Tony?" Beverly whispered.

I looked up and saw Beverly smile as she pointed to Sam and Sally. Beverly and I got up. I picked up Sally and Beverly picked up Sam and we brought them up to their bedrooms.

We went into Sam's bedroom and we put Sam to bed. Beverly kissed Sam on the forehead.

"Good night." Beverly whispered.

We left Sam's bedroom and closed the door.

I carried Sally to her bedroom and we put Sally to bed. Beverly kissed Sally on the forehead.

"Good night." Beverly whispered.

Beverly and I left Sally's bedroom and we closed the door. Beverly and I went into our bedroom and closed the door.

"So who do you think will find the pickle first?" I asked.

"That's a tough one because they both want it really bad." Beverly said.

"I just hope they don't destroy the tree looking for it." I said as I smiled.

"Yeah but think how much fun it's going to be watching them." Beverly said.

"You know what? Let's go put the Christmas pickle in the tree." I said.

"Okay." Beverly said.

Beverly and I went back downstairs to the living room.

"Now that the kids were sleeping, I can put the pickle ornament in the tree." I said.

"Make sure you hide it good." Beverly said.

"I will." I said as I sat on the floor next to the Christmas tree and placed the pickle ornament deep inside the tree.

"Is it hidden really good?" Beverly said.

"Yeah. They'll have a hard time finding it." I said.

Beverly looked in the tree. "I'm sure they will. I don't see it in there."

"That's good." I said.

"Are you ready to go up to bed now?" Beverly asked.

"Yes." I said.

"Oh, wait. I need to put the Christmas cookies out." Beverly went into the kitchen and got the elf cookies that Sally and her made and went back into the living room.

"Don't we have any chocolate chip cookies?" I asked.

"These are better than chocolate chip cookies because they're shaped like elves and Sally and I made them. They give it a Christmas feel." Beverly put the cookies onto a Christmas plate that was on the coffee table.

"Good idea. Hey, what about the milk?" I asked.

"Oh yeah, I almost forgot." Beverly went back into the kitchen and poured a glass of milk. She went back into the living room and placed the glass of milk next to the plate of cookies. "There, that's better."

"Are you ready to go up to bed? We don't want to be up when Santa came." I said with a smile.

"Sure." Beverly said.

Beverly and I went upstairs to our bedroom and got into bed.

"Good night." I said.

"Good night." Beverly said.

We kissed each other good night.

Chapter Ten

Whiskers was in the garbage can on the side of his house. The garbage can fell over and made a loud noise.

Sally woke up from the noise and looked out the window but she didn't see anything. Sally snuck into Sam's room. "Sam, wake up!" Sally yelled as she shook Sam.

"What's the matter?" Sam said in a groggy voice.

"I think Santa Claus is here!" Sally said with excitement.

"What were you talking about?" Sam asked.

"I heard a noise outside. I looked outside but I didn't see anything." Sally walked up to Sam's telescope by the window and looked through it.

"What were you doing?" Sam asked.

"Looking for Santa Claus." Sally said. Sally saw a red blinking light. "Look, it's Santa Claus! I can see Rudolph's red nose!"

Sam got up out of bed and pushed Sally out of the way and looked through the telescope. "That's not Santa Claus, that's an airplane." Sam went back to bed and pulled the covers over his head. "Now go back to bed."

Sally went back to her room and went back to bed.

Chapter Eleven

It was snowing at the North Pole. Santa's House and Santa's Workshop could be seen in the distance. "Santa Claus" was written on the mailbox out front.

Santa's elves were in the workshop making different Christmas ornaments. The elves were lined up along a conveyor belt.

Each elf had a different job putting different parts on the ornaments. Tinsel was the head elf. Dash was one of the elves on the production line.

"Okay elves, we need to get these ornaments done tonight for Santa." Tinsel said.

"We're working as hard as we can Tinsel." Dash said.

"Dash, you know that there can't be any mistakes especially tonight on Christmas Eve. Santa leaves in a few hours." Tinsel said.

Tinsel saw that some of the elf ornaments were missing their legs. "Stop the belt!!"

Dash ran over and pushed the emergency button to turn off the conveyor belt.

"What's wrong Tinsel? What's the matter?" Dash asked.

"What's wrong?! Look at these ornaments! They have no legs!" Tinsel said. "Who's in charge of the legs?"

All of the elves on the production line pointed to Twinkle Toes who was sleeping at his station.

"Twinkle Toes is, sir." Dash said.

"Twinkle Toes, wake up!!" Tinsel yelled.

Twinkle Toes woke up confused. "Who, what, where, what?"

"Twinkle Toes, why were you sleeping on the job? You know how important this job is." Tinsel said.

"Sorry, I was out late last night checking Santa's reindeer making sure that they were ready for tonight but there were some problems. I couldn't leave them the way they were." Twinkle Toes said.

"In that case, I'll forgive you this time but if you can't handle the job then I'll get someone else to replace you. Remember our motto, "no more, no less". We make every piece to order. If one is missing, someone is going to be disappointed." Tinsel said.

"Got it boss. I'll be fine. I won't let Santa down." Twinkle Toes said.

"Okay then, start the belt." Tinsel said.

Dash collected the ornaments with the missing legs and brought them over to Twinkle Toes. Dash started the conveyor belt and the conveyor belt began to move.

"Okay, let's get this done. Remember, it's for Santa and the children." Tinsel said.

Just then, Santa Claus entered the workshop. "So Tinsel, how's it going?" Santa asked.

"Hey Santa. Everything is on schedule and we'll be ready when you were ready to leave." Tinsel said.

"Good. I have a lot of extra presents to deliver this year. It seems that the children have been extra good this year." Santa said.

"Don't worry Santa, we won't let you down." Tinsel said.

At the end of the conveyor belt was Sparky, an elf who sprinkled pixie dust on the ornaments to make them come alive. Occasionally Sparky used the hose to shoot a little dust on an elf co-worker who laughed and thanked Sparky. Santa walked up to Sparky.

"Hey Santa. Would you like some happy dust?" Sparky asked.

"Ho Ho Ho. I couldn't be happier Sparky. How's it going?" Santa asked.

"It's going good Santa." Sparky noticed that he was getting low on pixie dust. "Hey, can someone get me some more pixie dust?"

"Coming right up." Tinsel saw Bling, one of the elves on the production line. "Bling, can you get a bag of pixie dust for Sparky?"

"Sure thing boss." Bling got a bag of pixie dust and gave it to Sparky.

"Thanks Bling." Tinsel said.

"Anytime." Bling said.

Bling went back to his station. Sparky opened the bag and poured it into the machine that sprayed the ornaments. Trixie, a female elf who was one of Santa's helpers came into the workshop.

"Excuse me Santa? Mrs. Claus is looking for you." Trixie said.

"Thank you Trixie. Tell her that I'll be there shortly." Santa said.

"Yes sir." Trixie left the workshop.

"Sparky, I want you to do me a favor." Santa Claus pulled out a golden pickle necklace. "Give this a good shot."

Sparky straightened up and aimed at Santa Claus's hand.

"Whoa Sparky, let me get out of the way first." Santa said.

"Okay. So, is that for Mrs. Claus?" Sparky asked.

"No, she's got as much cheer and good will as anyone can handle. This one is for a special child so fill it up with as much hope, joy, and happiness you can get in there." Santa said.

"But it's only one pickle."

"One pickle in the right hands will start a chain reaction that can spread around the world so make it a good one." Santa said.

"You got it Santa." Sparky blasted the pickle with so much pixie dust that the room began to get foggy. Sparky stopped spraying and giggled as he picked up the golden pickle and handed it to Santa Claus. "Wow, now that was awesome! I love my job."

"That's perfect. Thanks Sparky." Santa Claus took the pickle and put it in his pocket.

"Anytime Santa." Sparky said.

Santa turned to Tinsel. "I have to go see what the misses wants. Keep up the good work."

"Yes Santa." Tinsel said.

Santa Claus left the workshop and went into the kitchen. Mrs. Claus was in the kitchen.

"Trixie said you were looking for me?" Santa said.

"Santa, sit down. You need to eat before you go. The children don't want to see a skinny Santa." Mrs. Claus said.

"Mama, I'm fat already and I have to start getting ready to leave soon." Santa said.

"I still think you need to get a little bigger. Here, I got your suit ready for you." Mrs. Claus gave Santa his suit and shoes.

"Thank you mama." Santa said.

"You're welcome." Mrs. Claus said.

Miss L Toes, Twinkles Toes wife walked into the workshop.

"Wow, who's that?" Bling asked.

"That's my wife Miss L Toes." Twinkle Toes said.

"Really? You're a lucky guy." Bling said.

"Thanks."

Miss L Toes walked up to Twinkle Toes. "Hi Twinkle, what time were you getting off?"

"I should be done in about an hour." Twinkle Toes said.

"Okay, I have some decorations that need to be put up."

"Okay sure." Twinkle Toes said.

"Okay, I'll see you later." Miss L Toes said.

"Okay bye."

"Bye." Miss L Toes gave Twinkle Toes a kiss and left.

Outside Santa's Workshop was a garden of pickles. Ruby and Holly, two elves, were picking the pickles and putting them into a large cart.

"Hey Holly, there sure were a lot of pickles this year." Ruby said.

"Yes there is Ruby. Santa said that there have been a lot of children this year that were good so he wanted to do something special." Holly said.

"That's good that more and more children were being good. I was getting worried there for a while." Ruby said. "The past couple of years have been brutal."

"Yeah, you can tell that Santa's a lot jollier than usual." Holly said.

Ruby and Holly continued to fill the cart with pickles. After a while, the cart was filled.

"Okay, I don't think any more were going to fit. It's filled to the top." Ruby said.

"Okay. Give me a hand pushing the cart inside." Holly said.

Ruby and Holly pushed the cart into the workshop.

"Hey Tinsel, here's today's picking." Ruby said.

"Good. We were waiting for them. Push them into the detail room so they can get the ornament caps put on." Tinsel said.

"Yes sir." Ruby said.

Ruby and Holly pushed the cart into the detail room.

Junior, an elf, was at his station at the conveyor belt.

"Hey Junior. Here were the pickles." Ruby said.

"Thanks Ruby. Dump them right over there." Junior said.

Junior pointed to a table where elves were sitting at a table putting on the ornament caps and then placing them on a conveyor belt. Junior was at the end of the conveyor belt where he put on the final touches. Next to Junior was Angel, an elf putting the ornaments into boxes. Bing, an elf, put the labels on the boxes and placed them on a cart.

"Bing, this box of elf and snowman ornaments went to Milwaukee." Angel said.

"Okay Angel." Bing said.

"Bing, this box of nutcracker and pickle ornaments also went to Milwaukee. Santa said it's a priority." Angel said.

"Okay Angel." Bing put a label on the boxes and put it on a cart. After the cart was full, Bing brought it out to Santa's sled.

There were elves filling Santa's sled with presents. Bing put the ornaments in the sled. After Santa's sled was filled with the presents, Santa got in his sled.

"Now Dasher! Now Dancer! Now Prancer and Vixen! On Comet! On Cupid! On Donder and Blitzen! Now dash away! Dash away! Dash away!" Santa yelled.

Santa took off into the night. All of the elves cheered.

Chapter Twelve

The clock struck midnight at our house. Everyone was sleeping except me. I was watching television in my bedroom. I couldn't wait for the arrival of Santa Claus. I was like a little kid at Christmas.

The elf and snowman ornaments on my Christmas tree came to life. They were made at Santa's Workshop with pixie dust.

The elf and snowmen ornaments used the candy canes on the tree to climb up and down. Some of the elf and snowmen ornaments saw their reflection in the Christmas balls on the tree and made funny faces in the balls. The elf ornaments were Pixie, Candy Kane, Jingle, Jangle, Gizmo, Milo, Dooley, Winky, Binky, and Ginger. The snowmen ornaments were Jolly and Winter.

Gizmo was singing badly. "Silent night, holy night!"

Milo put his hands over his ears. "Gizmo, do you know why they call it Silent Night?"

Gizmo saw a toy car and got in it and started driving it. "Check it out! I'm driving!"

"Hey! Look out for the dog!" Milo yelled.

Gizmo almost hit Coco. Coco jumped up and ran away. Dooley saw a toy motorcycle.

"Check it out, a motorcycle!" Dooley got on the motorcycle and revved up the engine. Dooley took off and popped a wheelie. Dooley saw books set up like a ramp and drove up the ramp. Dooley yelled as he jumped over the coffee table. "Yeehaw!!"

Jingle saw a fruitcake on the table. "Hey, fruitcake!"

"Don't call me a fruitcake!" Jangle said.

"No not you, look, a fruitcake." Jingle pointed to the fruitcake.

"Sweet!" Jangle said.

Jingle and Jangle went over to the table and started eating the fruitcake. Jingle and Jangle saw the gingerbread house.

"Look, a gingerbread house!" Jingle said.

"Oh I love gingerbread!" Jangle said.

Jingle and Jangle walked over to the gingerbread house. Just as they were about to eat it, a gingerbread man came out of the house.

"Don't even think about it!" the gingerbread man yelled.

As Jingle and Jangle started to walk away, they grabbed some candy off of the house and ran.

"Hey, bring that back!" the gingerbread man yelled.

Jingle and Jangle kept running.

"Keep running and don't look back!" Jingle yelled.

Candy Kane and Ginger found a pair of shoes that belonged to Sally.

"Hey Ginger, do you want to jump rope?" Candy Kane asked.

"Sure." Ginger said.

Candy Kane and Ginger took the shoelaces out of the shoes and they jumped rope.

"This is fun!" Candy Kane said.

"Yes it is!" Ginger said.

Milo tripped over a wire and fell backwards. He bumped into a record player which started playing Christmas music. Candy Kane and Ginger stopped jump roping and started to dance.

Jingle and Jangle saw them dancing and danced along with them.

"Jangle, you dance pretty good." Jingle said.

"Thanks Jingle. You're not too bad either." Jangle said.

Dooley found the switch that turned on the train set around the base of the Christmas tree. Gizmo, Milo, Winky, and Binky saw the train moving and jumped on the train and rode it around and around. Binky saw a toy piano.

"Hey, look, a piano." Binky said.

Dooley stopped the train and the elves jumped off and walked over to the toy piano. They climbed up on the piano and jumped up and down on the keys to the melody of Jingle Bells.

They sang the song as they played it. "Jingle Bells, Jingle Bells, jingle all the way!"

Jingle and Jangle took some candy canes off of the tree and set up a Candy Cane Limbo game.

"Hey guys, come play the limbo game!" Jingle yelled.

"Yeah, see how low you can go!" Jangle yelled.

Candy Kane, Jolly, Winter, Gizmo, Milo, Dooley, Winky, and Binky walked over to the limbo game. They each took turns until one was left. Dooley was the last one to win the game. Winky looked across the room and saw iced cinnamon candles on a table. Pixie saw him and yelled but it was too late.

"Winky, no!" Pixie yelled.

Winky took a bite of the candle and then spit it out. "That doesn't taste too good."

"It's a candle Winky. You have to stop eating things that weren't food." Pixie said.

"Yeah but it looks so real." Winky said.

Binky walked up to a glass door and blew his breath on it to make it foggy and then drew a picture of a snowflake on it.

Milo walked up to a mousetrap near the couch along the wall and went to take the cheese off the mousetrap.

"Milo, look out for the mousetrap!" Pixie yelled.

Milo turned around to look at Pixie and bumped into the mousetrap. All of a sudden, the mouse trap closed slowly and played Christmas music.

"That was neat." Milo said.

The television went silent for a moment in my bedroom. I heard a noise coming from downstairs. I climbed out of bed and decided to find out where the noise was coming from.

Pixie heard someone coming down the stairs.

"Somebody's coming! Hurry, back on the tree!" Pixie yelled.

All of the elf ornaments climbed up the Christmas tree using the candy canes and they all got back to the spot where they were hanging except for Milo. He was too far away from the tree to get back up in the tree in time.

"Just lay there and stay still and everything will be fine." Pixie said.

"Okay." Milo said.

I went into the living room and saw one of the elf ornaments lying on the floor by the couch.

"Huh, I wonder how that got there." I said to myself. I looked at Coco. "Did you do this?" Coco turned his head sideways. He knew if he was guilty of something, I would be able to tell by his reactions.

"Did you do this?" I held the ornament near Coco and Coco turned his head sideways again.

I knew that Coco was innocent and picked up the ornament and hung the ornament back up on the tree.

"Good night Coco." He lifted his head and wagged his tail at me as I turned off the lights and went back to bed.

Chapter Thirteen

George, Margaret, and Amy were sleeping. The grandfather clock in their living room struck midnight. The nutcracker ornaments on the Christmas tree came to life. They too were made at Santa's Workshop with pixie dust. Heinz was the leader of the nutcrackers. The other nutcrackers were Schultzie, Bruno, Conrad, Fabian, Felix, Fritz, Gunther, Hugo, Jonas, Klaus, Leopold, Lucas, Oswald, Sebastian, Stefan, and Sven.

"Check it out, nuts!" Sven said.

Sven pointed to the bowl of almonds. The nutcracker ornaments climbed down the Christmas tree and went over to the coffee table.

"What's that?" Stefan saw the metal nutcracker on the table.

"That's an old fashioned nutcracker. As you know, we've improved since then." Heinz said.

"My grandfather used to tell me stories about those but I never saw one before." Stefan said.

"Yeah, they went out of style a long time ago." Heinz said.

The nutcracker ornaments sat around the bowl of almonds and cracked the almonds and ate them. The nutcracker ornaments told Christmas jokes to each other.

"Hey Hugo, why was Santa's helper depressed?" Klaus asked.

"I don't know, why?" Hugo asked.

"Because he had low elf-esteem." Klaus said.

"That was funny. Hey, what did the Christmas tree say to the ornament?" Felix asked.

"I don't know, what did he say?" Jonas asked.

"Aren't you tired of hanging around?" Felix asked.

"Wait, I got one. How much did Santa pay for his sleigh? Nothing, it was on the house." Fritz said.

"Oh yeah? What do snowmen eat for breakfast? Frosted Flakes." Bruno said.

"Where do snowmen keep their money? In a snow bank." Schultzie said.

"Why is Santa good at karate? Because he had a black belt." Lucas said.

"Why did the elf go to school? To learn his Elf-abet." Sebastian said.

"What do you get when you cross a snowman and a vampire? Frostbite." Leopold said.

"What is the difference between the ordinary alphabet and the Christmas alphabet? The Christmas alphabet had no L." Conrad said.

Klaus saw a bag of mini marshmallows. "Check it out, marshmallows!"

The nutcracker ornaments opened the bag.

"Let's roast them." Leopold said.

"How?" Klaus asked.

"Don't you guys know anything?" Heinz asked. "Take one of your rods and put the rod through the marshmallows. Be careful that you don't get too close to the fire otherwise you'll catch on fire."

"Gunther, let me see your rod." Klaus said.

"Okay, here." Gunther said.

Gunther handed Klaus his rod. Klaus took some of the marshmallows and pushed the rod through the marshmallows. He carefully walked to the fireplace making sure that he didn't get too close. Klaus saw a small piece of hot ash and placed the marshmallows over it.

"Now this is the way you roast marshmallows." Klaus said.

A hot ash sparked from the fireplace and flew towards Klaus and landed on his arm.

"Ow!! That's hot!" Klaus dropped the rod and brushed off the hot ash.

"Were you okay?" Heinz asked.

"Yeah, I'm good." Klaus said.

Gunther picked up the rod and finished roasting the marshmallows. When they were done, Gunther turned to the nutcracker ornaments.

"Come and get em!" Gunther yelled.

The nutcracker ornaments each took a marshmallow off of the rod and ate it.

"Now this is living the good life." Stefan said.

"It sure is." Gunther said.

Chapter Fourteen

The elf and snow ornaments came back to life in our house and Winky began to climb down the Christmas tree. Pixie saw Winky trying to sneak a cookie from the plate left out for Santa.

"Winky, get away from those cookies, they're for Santa!" Pixie yelled.

"Can't I just take a little bite?" Winky asked.

"No!" Pixie yelled.

Winky looked at the cookies and saw that they were shaped like elves. Winky had a surprised look on his face. He was speechless. Winky climbed back up the tree to the spot where he was hanging from and just hung there with a speechless look on his face.

"I told you. You keep trying to eat stuff that you're not supposed to. Maybe this time you'll learn not to do it anymore." Pixie said.

Pixie climbed up onto the table and checked the milk temperature with a candy cane thermometer. "Looks good." Pixie said to himself.

The ornaments were unaware that Whiskers entered the house through the doggy door and set off the jingles bells.

"Hey, did you guys hear that?" Binky asked.

"Hear what?" Winky asked.

The elf and snowman ornaments looked around but they didn't see anything. Binky listened again but didn't hear anything.

"I guess it was nothing." Binky said.

Whiskers entered the living room and hid from the ornaments as he cautiously walked over to the Christmas tree. Whiskers got to the Christmas tree without being seen. He cautiously climbed up the tree and took the Christmas pickle ornament off of the tree. Pixie heard a noise coming from inside the Christmas tree. Pixie looked inside and saw Whiskers take the Christmas pickle.

"Hey, put that back!" Pixie yelled.

All of the ornaments heard Pixie yell and turned to see what was going on.

"Hey!" the ornaments yelled.

Pixie pulled the pin that connected him to the hook. As Pixie was falling from the tree, Pixie jumped onto Whisker's back as he was getting away. Pixie tried to hold on but Whiskers knocked him off and Pixie fell on the floor.

"Frostbite!" Pixie said.

Whiskers ran out of the house and took the Christmas pickle ornament back to his house. Candy Kane jumped down from the tree.

"Pixie, were you okay?" Candy Kane asked.

"Yeah, I'm okay. He took the Christmas pickle ornament." Pixie said.

"I know." Candy Kane said.

"We have to get it back. The children will be disappointed if we don't." Pixie said.

"You're right. We have to get it back no matter what the price is." Candy Kane said.

Pixie looked up the tree. "Everyone, come down here!"

The elf and snowman ornaments climbed down and gathered around the bottom of the Christmas tree.

"Okay, listen up. We have to get that ornament back." Pixie said.

"But how?" Jingle asked.

"We need to make a plan. Everyone grab a sled ornament and head to the backyard." Pixie said.

The elf and snowman ornaments took the sled ornaments that were hanging on the tree. They went into the kitchen and walked through the doggy door out to the backyard.

The ornaments went outside. It was snowing lightly.

"Pixie, how do we even know where the Christmas pickle is?" Jingle asked.

"I'll show you." Pixie made a snowball. The snowball turned into a crystal ball. "It's called Christmas magic." Pixie looked at the crystal ball and saw the Christmas pickle hanging on the Klinger's Christmas tree next door. "The ornaments next door have it."

Jingle saw an ice puddle and tried to skate on it but couldn't with the shoes that he had on. He saw a couple of paper clips on the ground and tied them to his shoes.

"Check it out! I'm skating!"

Pixie saw Jingle trying to skate. "Will you knock it off? We need to get the Christmas pickle back!"

"Sorry." Jingle took off the paper clips.

"Okay, everyone gather around." Pixie drew a map of the two houses and their properties in the snow. "This is our house and this is where the ornament is." Pixie pointed at the map. "We were going to use the toy trucks to get over to their yard."

They walked over to the monster trucks, the Tonka trucks, and the fire truck toys that belonged to Sam.

"Who's gonna drive them Pixie?" Dooley asked.

"I'll drive the dump truck, Milo will drive the monster truck and Gizmo will drive the fire truck. Some of you will ride in the back of the trucks. The rest of you will have to walk." Pixie said.

The elf ornaments that had to walk turned their boots into skis.

"Darn." Dooley said.

"Okay, let's go!" Pixie yelled.

Some of the elf ornaments climbed into the trucks. Pixie used Christmas magic to start the trucks.

As they drove the trucks over to the yard next door, it began to snow more heavily. They turned the windshield wipers on the trucks. The ornaments and the toys left imprints in the snow but were covered up quick from the falling snow. All of a sudden, the spotlight that lit up the back yard went out.

"I can't see anything with this snow falling!" Milo yelled.

"Turn on the fog lights!" Pixie yelled.

Milo turned the fog lights on and the lights lit up the way.

Pixie looked up and saw icicles falling from a tree towards Dooley. "Look out Dooley!!"

Dooley looked up and saw the icicles falling and jumped out of the way.

"Wow that was close!" Dooley said.

"Were you okay?" Pixie asked.

"Yes, thanks." Dooley said.

The ornaments continued to drive through the back yard towards the Klinger's house. Winky saw a big candy cane sticking out of the ground but didn't know it was a metal pole decorated as a candy cane. Winky stuck his tongue out and licked the pole and his tongue got stuck on the metal pole.

"Winky, what did I tell you about that?" Pixie asked.

"Sorry Pixie. I can't get my tongue off of the candy cane. I'm stuck." Winky said talking funny.

Pixie stopped the dump truck and got out.

"C'mon, help me get him unstuck." Pixie and some of the ornaments pulled on Winky and they got him off of the pole.

"Now get in the truck so I can keep my eye on you." Pixie said to Winky.

"Fine." Winky said talking funny.

Winky got into the dump truck. The ornaments continued on their journey. There were several mounds of snows that they drove up and over.

Ginger sunk in one of the snow banks. Pixie saw what happened and stopped the truck. Binky ran over to her.

"Hey, were you okay?" Binky asked.

Ginger shivered as she climbed out of the snow bank. "Yeah, just cold."

"C'mon, pull her out!" Pixie yelled.

Three elf ornaments pulled Ginger out of the snow.

"Binky, I need you to make a fire to warm her up." Pixie said.

"A fire? I can't make a fire." Binky said.

"Winter and I can make an igloo." Jolly said. "That will keep her warm."

"I'll be fine." Ginger said.

"Nonsense. They'll help you get warm and then you guys can catch up." Pixie said.

"Okay." Ginger said.

The snowmen ornaments made an igloo. The rest of the elf ornaments continued on the journey. The elf ornaments with the sleds slid down the mounds of snow. When they reached the edge of the yard, there were bushes that separated the two yards. They drove under the bushes into the Klinger's yard.

The ornaments drove through the yard right up to the back door of the Klinger's house.

"How do we get in?" Dooley asked.

Chapter Fifteen

All of a sudden, the back door opened. Whiskers came out of the house. The ornaments hid from Whiskers as they leaned up against the house. Whiskers didn't see the ornaments. Pixie put a stick between the door and the wall to prevent the door from closing all the way shut. Whiskers walked through the yard.

The elf and snowman ornaments entered the house and walked through the kitchen into the living room.

Pixie saw the Christmas pickle ornament hanging on the Christmas tree. It was hanging next to Heinz.

"Hey, get out of here! Go back home where you belong!" Heinz yelled.

"That's our Christmas pickle ornament and you know it!" Pixie said.

"Finders keepers is what I always say." Heinz said.

"Give it back!" Pixie said.

"Give it back or what?" Heinz asked.

"Give it back or fight!" Pixie said.

"Fight? Fight who? You? At least give me a challenge. Don't you see my big brothers on top of the fireplace mantle?" Heinz asked.

Pixie looked over and saw the big nutcracker statues. The nutcracker statues on the fireplace mantle came to life.

"Sorry but we're not going to help you. This is your battle not ours." the big brother nutcracker said.

"Some brother you were." Heinz said.

"C'mon, let's take it outside and have a snowball fight." Pixie said.

"Sounds good to me. I haven't had a good snowball fight in a long time." Heinz said.

"Let's do it! To the backyard!" Pixie yelled.

"Let's go men!" Heinz yelled.

All of the ornaments went out to the backyard and gathered on the porch. Pixie explained the rules.

"If you get knocked down, you're out. The last team standing wins." Pixie said.

"Get ready to lose, loser." Heinz said.

The ornaments went out on the lawn and set up barricades on each side using tree branches and hiding behind the toy trucks.

"Is everyone ready? It's jingle time!" Pixie yelled.

The nutcrackers with drums did a drum roll. The snowball fight began. Ginger didn't fight so she kept score of the fight.

"Let's gang up on some of the nutcrackers." Pixie said.

All of the elf and snowman ornaments threw snowballs at a group of nutcrackers.

"Hey, that's not fair!" Heinz yelled.

"Fair? Hello? It's a fight." Pixie said.

Pixie turned to the snowmen. "You snowmen are really good."

"What did you expect? We're made of snow." Jolly said.

The ornaments continued with the snowball fight. Some of the ornaments slid down a snow bank and threw snowballs on their way down. Some of the nutcrackers climbed a tree and shook a branch. The snow dropped on some of the elf ornaments and buried them in the snow.

As the fight went on, along came Whiskers. He began to pounce on some of the ornaments trying to capture them. The elf ornaments ran and hid under the bushes. The snowmen blended into the mounds of snow. The nutcracker ornaments stood still. They knew that Whiskers won't see them if they were still. The nutcrackers knew that they can't hide as well in the snow as the snowmen. They were easy targets with their colorful uniforms.

"We got to get rid of that cat, but how?" Jangle asked.

"I know. I saw a toy mouse in our yard. I'll go back and tie it to the monster truck to distract him." Milo said.

Milo went back to our yard and tied the toy mouse to the truck and returned back.

Milo saw Whiskers trying to pounce on the elf ornaments. "Yo cat? Yeah you, you ornament thief. Come and get me!" Milo threw a snowball to get Whisker's attention. Milo started the truck and began to pull the toy mouse on the rope that was attached. He drove wildly through the yard trying to avoid the other elf and snowmen ornaments. Whiskers pounced on the snow trying to capture the mouse.

While the elf ornaments were distracted watching Whiskers, Heinz snuck into the house and got the almond shells, then found a rubber band and got the metal nutcracker and made a sling shot and used the metal nutcracker to shoot shells at the elf and snowmen ornaments.

Gizmo put the fire truck hose in ice puddles. He broke the ice then used pixie magic. The fire truck could now pump water through the hose. The elf ornaments used the fire truck hose to freeze the nutcrackers in place.

Heinz went outside and used the metal nutcracker sling shot that kept the elf and snowmen ornaments behind the trucks and limited their attack. Heinz's plan was successful. He was holding the elf and snowmen ornaments back so the frozen nutcrackers could break free.

"What were we going to do? We got the cat out of the yard with the mouse but now we're still stuck hiding behind the trucks. The nutcrackers have us pinned down with the shells." Binky said.

Suddenly Milo arrived with the monster truck back in the yard minus the mouse. "I'm back. I finally let the cat catch the mouse. At least he won't bother us anymore tonight."

"Hurry, place the truck to block the shells that were holding us down!" Pixie yelled.

"No I got an idea. I still have the rope. I'll lasso the leader who is shooting the shells." Milo said.

Milo quickly drove up alongside of Heinz. He lassoed him with the rope putting him behind the truck to the cheering elf and snowmen ornaments. The other nutcrackers tried to reset the metal nutcracker sling shot but were pounded with snowballs from the snowmen ornaments. The battle continued until it was obvious that the nutcrackers were tired. After a short time, the elf and snowmen ornaments won the snowball fight. Heinz was now confronted by the elf ornaments.

"We won! Now give me the pickle!" Pixie said.

"Yeah, you guys crumbled like a Christmas cookie." Milo said.

"Ok but let me go first." Heinz said.

"No, not until we walk you over with the white flag." Pixie said.

The elf ornaments marched Heinz with the white flag across the yard with the lasso still on. The nutcrackers saw the defeat.

"Oh well, we tried. They had a better plan." Sven said.

Heinz and the elf ornaments went inside and Heinz climbed up the tree and took the Christmas pickle off the tree and handed it to Pixie.

"Well, you won fair and square. Here's your reward." Heinz gave Pixie the Christmas pickle ornament. Pixie and Heinz shook hands. "Next time the victory will be ours."

"Don't count on it, we always improvise, adapt, and overcome!" Pixie said.

The elf and snowmen ornaments walked away in triumph, carrying the precious pickle ornament.

"Okay gang, let's get this back to the house before the children wake up." Pixie said.

Pixie put the Christmas pickle ornament in the back of the dump truck and drove it back to our house. The elf ornaments that were in the back of the truck now have to walk back except for a few that were in the truck holding the Christmas pickle ornament.

Chapter Sixteen

The elf and snowmen ornaments were in the Christmas tree.

"Where are we gonna put the pickle ornament in the tree?" Jingle asked.

"We have to put the pickle ornament back in the same spot." Pixie said.

"Pixie, it was right here." Candy Kane pointed to the branch where it was hanging from.

Pixie put the Christmas pickle ornament on the tree. "Everybody did a great job. I'm so proud of everyone."

All of the ornaments applauded each other. Just then, jingle bells could be heard in the distance.

"Look!" Jingle said pointing outside.

A glowing red light could be seen in the distance.

"It's Santa! Everyone, back to your places!" Pixie yelled.

All of the ornaments went back to their places.

Santa Claus landed on our roof. Santa got out of the sled and went down the chimney.

Santa put presents under the tree and then put a blue velvet bag under the tree. Santa saw the cookies and milk left on the table. He began to eat the elf shaped cookies.

Winky saw Santa eating the cookies and fell off the tree. Santa turned around and saw Winky lying on the floor.

"It's okay Winky, they're not real elves. They were made for me." Santa said.

"That's a relief." Winky said.

Santa Claus turned to Pixie. "I'm proud of you guys. Good job getting the bag back."

"Thanks Santa." Pixie said.

Santa drank the milk and then walked to the fireplace.

"Merry Christmas!" Santa said.

"Merry Christmas to you too." Pixie said.

Santa went up the chimney. Santa got into his sled and went next door to the Klinger house.

Santa Claus landed on the Klinger house roof. Santa got out of the sled and went down the chimney.

Santa put presents under the tree.

"You guys got a beating tonight, didn't you?" Santa said.

"Yes we did Santa." Heinz said.

"I'm not happy about what happened. That pickle is for a special child." Santa said. "Don't let it happen again."

"Yes Santa." Heinz said.

Santa saw the cookies and milk left on the table. He ate the cookies and drank the milk then went up the chimney. Santa got into his sled and left.

Chapter Seventeen

It was Christmas morning. Sally woke up and went into Sam's room.

"Sam! Wake up! It's Christmas!" Sally yelled.

Sam got out of bed and was already in his pajamas. Sam and Sally ran down the stairs to the living room.

Sam and Sally went into the living room with Coco behind them. Shortly after, Beverly and I came down the stairs.

"C'mon Sally, let's look for the pickle." Sam said.

"Be careful with the tree." I said.

"We will." Sam and Sally said.

Sam and Sally looked for the Christmas pickle ornament lifting the branches and moving them out of the way. Pixie pushed the Christmas pickle ornament towards Sally's hand so she could find it easier. After a while, Sally found the Christmas pickle ornament.

"I found it! I found it!" Sally yelled with excitement.

The elf and snowmen ornaments saw Sally's face light up when she found the Christmas pickle ornament.

They knew that the expression on her face was well worth it.

"Good for you Sally!" Beverly said.

Beverly, Sam, Sally, and I gathered around the Christmas tree. There were two large presents off to the side. One had Sam's name on it and the other one had Sally's name on it.

"Open those first." I pointed to the presents.

Sam and Sally ripped off the Christmas paper and saw two brand new bikes.

"This is what I asked Santa for! I asked him for a bike for me and Sam." Sally said.

"That's because you were good this year. Santa knows when you're good or bad." I said.

Sally and Sam got on their bikes and started to ride the bikes in the house.

"Don't ride them in the house kids. They're for outside. Besides, there were still more presents to open." I said.

"Okay Daddy." Sally said.

Sam and Sally got off of their bikes and sat back down by the Christmas tree. It had already been the best Christmas ever but more was still to come. The whole bottom of the tree was stuffed with red and green wrapped packages of all sizes. Gold and silver satin bows glowed in the tree lights and the ornaments shined under the tinsel and garland.

"Kids, why don't you start handing out the presents?" I asked.

"Okay Dad." Sam and Sally said.

A big box was handed to Beverly. She opened it up. There was a large bag inside.

"Oh Tony, you outdid yourself this year. I can't believe you got me this bag. It's so beautiful. You can't find these anywhere. The shelves have been empty for months." Beverly said.

"I didn't get that. That was from Santa Claus." I said.

"Really?" Sally asked.

"What, you think Santa got presents just for kids? Santa's for everyone." I said.

"I know Daddy." Sally said.

More presents such as toys and clothes were handed out as well as more smiles and laughter filled the room.

"Tony, do you want any eggnog?" Beverly asked.

"What's that?" Sam asked.

"It's yummy but it may be too adult for you." I said.

"I think it would be okay as long as they don't have too much." Beverly said.

"Okay." I said.

"What about you Sally? Do you want to try it?" Beverly asked.

"I don't know. Will I like it?" Sally asked.

"You'll never know unless you try it. I'll get you both a sip to try." Beverly said.

"Is it made out of eggs?" Beverly asked.

"No, it's just a name. Try it and if you don't like it then you don't have to drink it." Beverly said.

Beverly went into the kitchen and then returned with a carton and four glasses.

"Wow, we had a big Christmas this year but I think there is one more present left." I said.

"I think we got them all. I don't see any more presents." Sam said.

"Isn't there a blue velvet bag all the way in the back?" I asked.

"Oh yeah, I see it but I can't reach it. It's too far under the tree." Sam said.

"Well, maybe it was meant for Sally to get it." Beverly said.

"For me? Are you sure?" Sally asked.

"It's the last present. It's the extra present for finding the Christmas pickle and you're the only one small enough to reach it." I said.

"Sally, just scoot under there and see what you got." Beverly said.

Sally settled herself down on the carpet and slipped under the tree without effort. Sally grabbed the blue velvet bag. It was small and something felt like a rock inside.

The gold silk cord on the end wrapped around her fingers and she backed out of the tree as easily as she got under it.

"Let me see! Let me see!" Sam said as he almost knocked over his eggnog.

"Sam, watch your eggnog." Beverly said.

"You know that you can never tell what the Christmas pickle is going to bring. Sally, what did you get?" I asked.

Sally pulled on the silk string and reached inside. She felt something. Something warm, something friendly, something Sally knew that will touch her heart. She would treasure this for the rest of her life. Sally took out a golden pickle necklace from the blue velvet bag.

"That's beautiful!" Beverly said.

"Bev, did you?" I asked.

"No, I thought you did." Beverly said.

"I got her something but it wasn't that." I said.

"It's just a pickle on a necklace." Sam said.

"It's a gold pickle on a gold necklace. I don't know why but I feel that it means something special." Sally offered the pickle to Sam who hesitated at first but then held out his hand.

"I thought that the bicycles were the best gifts I ever got but Sally's right, there is something different about it." Sam said.

Sam handed me the pickle necklace. I knew that I had never seen it before but can also feel something special about it as well. I passed it to Beverly. She was just as mystified as I was.

"It's the best pickle gift I've ever seen. Here, let me put it on you." Beverly said.

Sally moved over to Beverly. Sally sat in front of Beverly as Beverly put the necklace on her.

"Thanks Mom!" Sally said.

"You're welcome!" Beverly said.

Later on that night, the elf and snowmen ornaments had a Christmas party with music and dancing. Mistletoe was hanging from the bottom of the tree for the elf ornaments. Candy Kane put on a hat with a mistletoe hanging on it.

"Oh Pixie?" Candy Kane asked.

Pixie turned around and looked at Candy Kane. Candy Kane pointed to the mistletoe and gave him a big kiss.

Sam and Sally grew up, as kids will do. Sam got married and had kids of his own. Sally grew up into a beautiful woman who worked with many charities, helping hundreds and thousands of people. She never removed the necklace around her neck.

Made in the USA
San Bernardino, CA
11 December 2014